Plants

 HOUGHTON MIFFLIN   BOSTON

Number of Words: 326

Printed in China

ISBN-13: 978-0-618-75907-1
ISBN-10: 0-618-75907-7

123456789-NPC-12 11 10 09 08 07 06

Contents

1 What Are the Parts of Plants?

Plants have parts.
Plants have roots, stems,
and leaves.
Some plants have flowers.
Each part helps
in a different way.

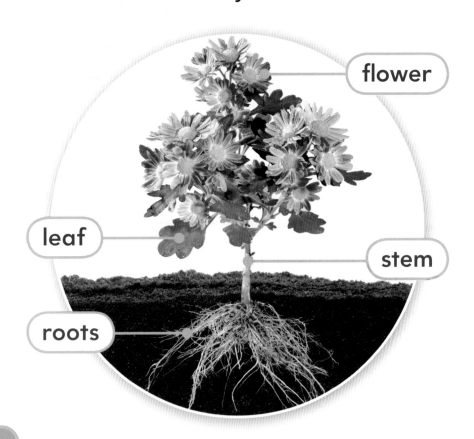

flower

leaf

stem

roots

Roots and Stems

Roots take in water.
Roots hold the plant
in the ground.
A **stem** joins parts of plants.
Stems carry water from the roots
to other parts.
Stems hold the plant up.

Leaves

Most plants have leaves.
Leaves make food for the plant.
Leaves also make oxygen.
People and animals need oxygen.

Flowers and Seeds

Many plants have flowers.

A **flower** makes seeds.

A **seed** has a new plant inside it.

New plants grow from seeds.

seeds

Draw Conclusions

Why are seeds important?

2 How Can Plants Be Sorted?

You can sort plants.
You can put plants in groups.
You can sort plants
by their parts.
Some plants have sharp points
called **spines**.

spines

Some plants have flowers.
Some plants have flat leaves.

flat leaf

Eating Plants

Some plants are food for people.
You can buy food plants
in a store.
These plants are safe to eat.
Not all plants are safe to eat.

Some plants are food for animals.

Draw Conclusions

How do plants help animals?

3 How Do Plants Change as They Grow?

Pine trees start as seeds.
Pine seeds are in a **cone**.
A seed grows into a plant
called a **seedling**.
The seedling grows into a tree.

cone

seedling

The tree grows cones.
Seeds are in the cones.
Pine trees start as seeds!

Plant Life Cycles

Plants change as they grow.
Changes in plants and animals
happen in an order
called a **life cycle**.

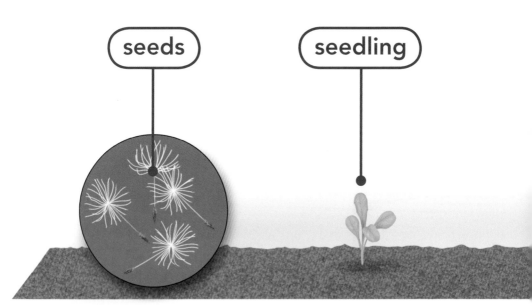

seeds

seedling

Plant Lives

Different plants have different life cycles.
Some plants have long life cycles.
Some plants have short life cycles.

Sequence

What comes after the seed in a plant's life cycle?

growing plant

flowers grow

new seeds

Glossary

cone The part of a pine tree where seeds grow.

flower The part of a plant that makes seeds.

leaf Part of a plant that makes food for the plant.

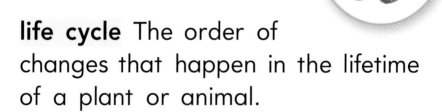

life cycle The order of changes that happen in the lifetime of a plant or animal.

roots The parts of the plant that take in water from the ground.

Glossary

seed The part of a plant that has a new plant inside it.

seedling A young plant.

spines Sharp points on a cactus.

stem Part of a plant that connects the roots to the other plant parts.

Think About What You Have Read

❶ A _____ makes seeds.

A) stem

B) flower

C) spine

D) root

❷ How do stems help a plant?

❸ What is one way to group plants?

❹ What happens in a plant's life cycle after it flowers?